ELLA McKEEN, KICKBALL QUEEN

BETH MILLS

CAROLRHODA BOOKS
Minneapolis

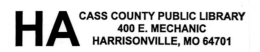

TO MOM AND DAD,
FOR EVERYTHING

Carolrhoda Books
A division of Lerner Publishing Group, Inc.
241 First Avenue North
Minneapolis, MN 55401 USA

For reading levels and more information, look up this title at www.lernerbooks.com.

Designed by Danielle Carnito.
Main body text set in Mikado Medium 15/23.
Typeface provided by HVD Fonts.
The illustrations in this book were painted digitally.

Library of Congress Cataloging-in-Publication Data

Names: Mills, Beth, 1986- author, illustrator.
Title: Ella McKeen, kickball queen / Beth Mills.
Description: Minneapolis : Carolrhoda Books, [2019] | Summary: When first-grader Ella, the undisputed kickball queen at school, is bested by new student Riya Patel, she throws a tantrum with her entire class watching.
Identifiers: LCCN 2018038599 (print) | LCCN 2018043263 (ebook) | ISBN 9781541561052 (eb pdf) | ISBN 9781541528970 (lb : alk. paper)
Subjects: | CYAC: Kickball—Fiction. | Sportsmanship—Fiction. | Schools—Fiction. | Behavior—Fiction.
Classification: LCC PZ7.1.M5897 (ebook) | LCC PZ7.1.M5897 El 2019 (print) | DDC [E]—dc23

LC record available at https://lccn.loc.gov/2018038599

Manufactured in the United States of America
2-49475-35701-7/30/2020

When **Ella McKeen** steps up to the plate, everyone knows what to do: "MOVE BACK! MOVE BACK!"

Ella smiles at Kyle Sultana, the pitcher. Ella smiles at her classmates on the field. Her kicks have never been caught.

Not the **ZINGER.**

Not the **bouncer.**

And **definitely** not the B O M B.

The ball arcs through the air, higher and higher until it is lost in the sun. The outfielders groan. **It's a home run for sure!**

But then . . .

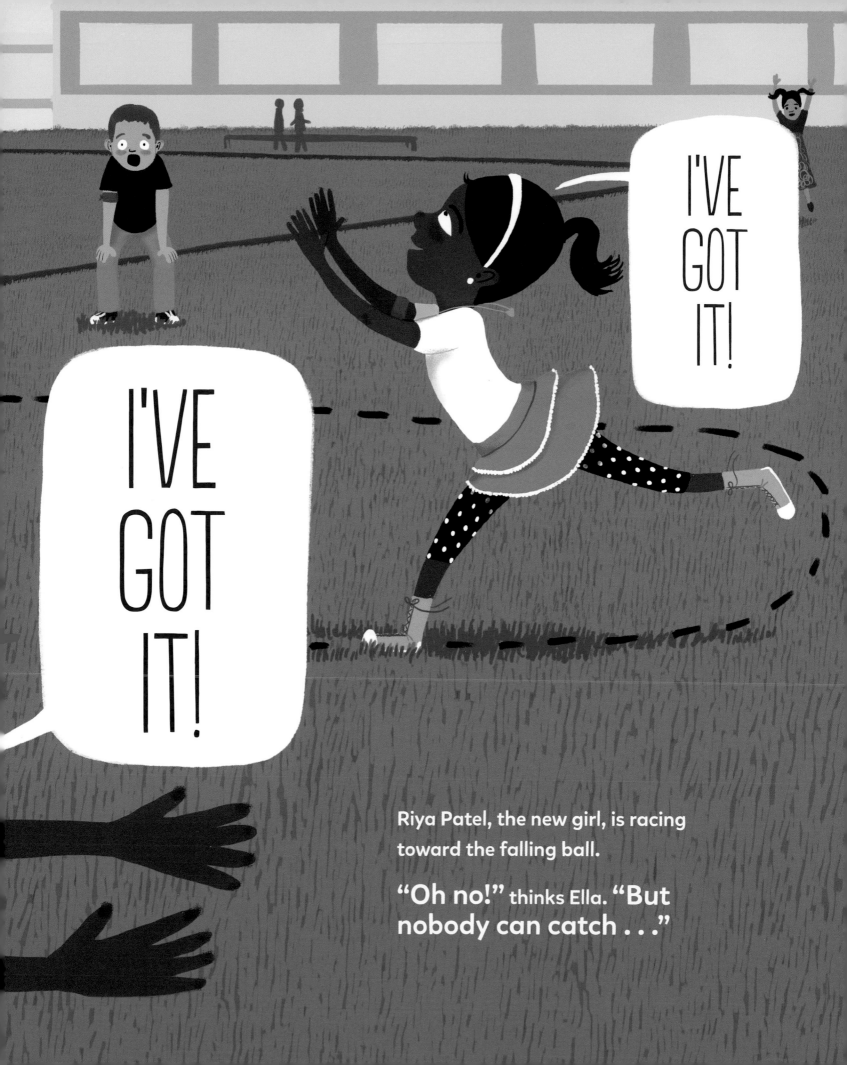

Riya Patel, the new girl, is racing toward the falling ball.

"Oh no!" thinks Ella. "But nobody can catch . . ."

"**WOW!** What a great catch!" yells Kyle. Everyone starts cheering—even Ella's own team!

Ella's stomach drops to her feet.
Her hands clench into fists.

She feels a twisty, turn-y,
terrible burning in her chest.

Her cheeks get hot,

her eyes fill with tears, and . . .

NO! THAT'S
THAT'S MY BEST
CAN CATCH THE BOM
TO BE OUT! I WAN
I WAS GOING TO
THAT'S NOT FAIR
SUPPOSED TO DO
EVERYTHING! I DO
DON'T WANT TO PLA
I'M THE BEST! NOT
TO LOSE! I NEVE

Ella suddenly stops. It is very quiet. There is no more cheering. There is no more talking. There is no more noise anywhere . . .

and everyone is looking at her.

Ella feels like crawling under home plate and staying there forever.

Nobody hears her over the end-of-recess bell.

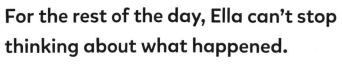

For the rest of the day, Ella can't stop thinking about what happened.

And Riya.

And how everyone stared.

And how she wanted to hide.

Ella thinks about going to
school in the morning.

And she feels even worse.

The next morning, Ella is pretty sure everyone is avoiding her. And she tries not to even look at Riya. But on the way to recess, Ella's stomach starts to drop—she will have to see Riya on the field.

The captains start to pick teams. Ella knows she has to say something. She takes a deep breath and jogs over to Riya.

"Look, I'm sorry for yesterday. That catch was really good. But I'm the Kickball Queen here. Nobody's ever caught any of my kicks before."

"Well, OK." says Riya. "But you should know, I was the Kickball Queen at my old school, definitely the best, and I can catch anything. So you'd better watch out."

"Really?" replies Ella.
"We'll see about that."

Riya smiles and says,

"CHALLENGE ACCEPTED."

At the top of the second inning, Riya catches the Bouncer after only two bounces and tags Ella out as she rounds second.

Ella's stomach drops to her feet.

Her hands clench into fists.

She feels a twisty,
turn-y, terrible
burning in her chest.

Her cheeks get hot,

her eyes fill with tears, and . . .

Ella takes a deep breath.

She walks up to Riya and says . . .

As Ella runs back to the bench, she thinks,
"I wonder if Riya could catch the Zinger . . ."